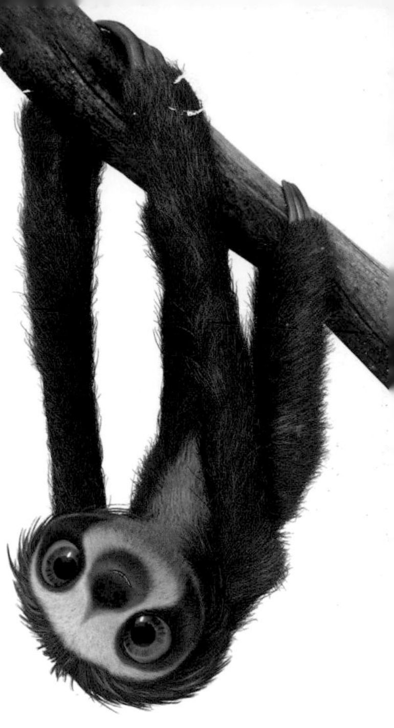

HERE COME THE CROODS

DreamWorks

D1434153

H46 618 696 0

THE CROODS: HERE COME THE CROODS
A BANTAM BOOK 978 0 857 51243 7
Published in Great Britain by Bantam, an imprint of Random House Children's Publishers UK
A Random House Group Company.

This edition published 2013

1 3 5 7 9 10 8 6 4 2

The Croods © 2013 DreamWorks Animation L.L.C.

All rights reserved. No part of this publication may be reproduced, stored in a retrieval system,
or transmitted in any form or by any means, electronic, mechanical, photocopying,
recording or otherwise, without the prior permission of the publishers.

Bantam Books are published by Random House Children's Publisher's UK,
61–63 Uxbridge Road, London W5 5SA

www.**randomhousechildrens**.co.uk

Addresses for companies within The Random House Group Limited can be found at:
www.randomhouse.co.uk/offices.htm

THE RANDOM HOUSE GROUP Limited Reg. No. 954009

A CIP catalogue record for this book is available from the British Library

Printed in Italy

The Random House Group Limited supports the Forest Stewardship Council (FSC®), the leading international
forest certification organization. Our books carrying the FSC label are printed on FSC®-certified paper.
FSC is the only forest certification scheme endorsed by the leading environmental organizations, including
Greenpeace. Our paper procurement policy can be found at www.randomhouse.co.uk/environment.

Meet the Croods.

They are cavemen, but they won't be for much longer. Their world is about to change!

This is Grug. He is the leader of the Croods.

Grug lives by three rules.

Anything new is bad.

Curiosity is bad.

Going out at night is bad.

He tells his family to always be afraid.

Grug is very strong, and he loves his family very much. He will do anything to keep them safe.

This is Eep. She is Grug's oldest daughter.

Eep doesn't like her father's rules. She wants to meet new people, see new sights and go on new adventures.

Grug reminds her
that anything new
is bad.

When their cave collapses, the Croods are forced to journey into a whole new world.

Eep is excited. So is her younger brother, Thunk.

Thunk wants to be strong,
just like his dad.

He is always eager to hunt,
help or tuck in! He just doesn't
like it when Gran tries to tuck in
to him!

This new world is filled with
new creatures.
Some of them look cute, like fuzzy
little Bear Pears.

And some of them are dangerous, like Punch Monkeys.

When Grug first encounters a group of Punch Monkeys, they hit him back and forth, as if he's a pinball in a pinball machine!

And some creatures are just
plain scary, like Piranhakeets.

A swarm of them can eat an entire Land Whale in a matter of seconds!

The Croods discover new things
everywhere in this new world.
They don't always know what to do.

Eep decides it's time to call
someone who can help.

Who does she call? Guy!
When the Croods meet Guy,
he is living by himself. He survives
by inventing things that help him to
stay safe . . .

. . . like a belt to hold his trousers up, shoes to walk across spiky coral and fire to cook food and scare dangerous creatures away.

Grug doesn't think the family needs Guy's help. But Gran reminds him that they need Guy's fire.

Grug agrees to bring him along on the Croods' journey.

Gran is the oldest Crood.
She wears a dress made out
of a lizard's skin. The dress even
has a tail!

Gran is not a big fan of baths.
She doesn't like losing her
protective layer of dirt and bugs.
   She is also not a big fan of Grug,
but deep down she loves him.

Grug's wife is called Ugga. She always has her hands full taking care of Sandy.

Sandy is the youngest Crood.
She is always running everywhere
and getting into everything!
Sandy might be little, but
she's fearless.

As the Croods continue on their journey to find a new cave on the mountain, they see many more things that are new to them . . .

. . . like popcorn.
   At first Grug doesn't want
his family to eat the popcorn
because it's new. But they do,
and it's delicious!

The Croods also learn new things. Guy teaches them how to construct a trap to catch a Turkeyfish.

Guy and Eep lure the Turkeyfish into the trap with a puppet.

The Croods learn that cooked Turkeyfish tastes better than raw bugs.

When the Croods finally make it
to the mountain, it starts to crumble!
Everyone wants to hide in a cave for
safety . . . everyone except Grug.
He has changed. He doesn't want
his family to be afraid of new things
anymore.

He tells them to follow the light.
And they do!

Grug uses his strength and his new ideas to help him and his family get to the other side of the mountain.

Now the Croods live on the beach, where they can enjoy tomorrow!